Disney PRINCESS

Belle's Perfect Day

PaRragon

Bath · New York · Cologne · Melbourne · Delhi
Hong Kong · Shenzhen · Singapore

Belle's wedding was just days away. "I'm so happy!" Belle told Mrs Potts. "The Prince has done so much for me. I want to make our wedding a special celebration. We need to show him how much we appreciate him and how well-loved he is."

"What a wonderful idea, my dear!" said Mrs Potts.

Belle thought back to when she first arrived at the castle. It was very frightening – everyone was under a magical spell. The Prince had become an angry beast and the servants were enchanted objects.

But over time, Belle became friends with the servants.
Then she fell in love with the Beast.
The whole household became a family.

Belle smiled at her friends. "It will mean so much to him to have you all there!" she said. "I know you all want to help with the preparations, but you must also help by being our guests."

Mrs Potts and the other servants worked hard to prepare for the big day.

They were determined to show the couple how much they loved them.

Meanwhile, the Prince was preparing for the wedding, too.
"I am the happiest man in the world!" he declared to Lumiere
and Cogsworth. "And I want Belle to be the happiest woman!"

The Prince fell silent as he remembered meeting Belle. Back then, he thought that she could never love a hideous beast.

But Belle spent time getting to know the Beast. Later on, she chose to return to the castle – and to him – when she could have left forever.

When she declared her
love, the spell was broken!

"How can I show Belle how much I love her?" the Prince asked. "I know! Let's find a special gift for her in the village!" Lumiere and Mrs Potts wondered how they could show their love and appreciation for the young couple, too.

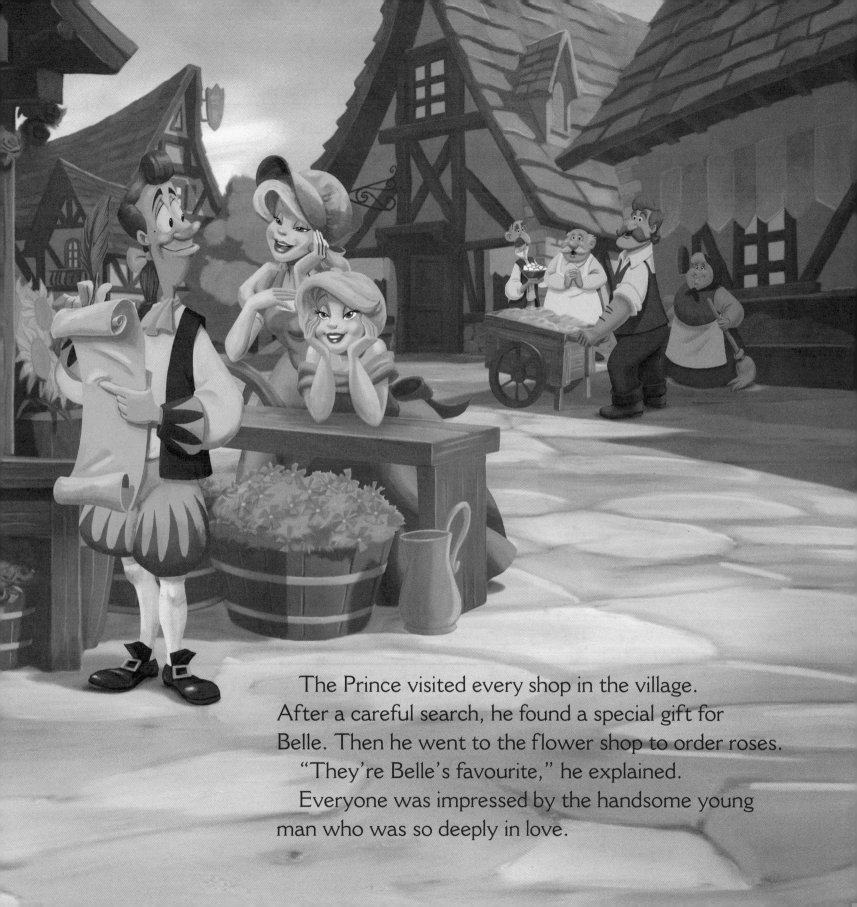

The Prince visited every shop in the village.
After a careful search, he found a special gift for
Belle. Then he went to the flower shop to order roses.
"They're Belle's favourite," he explained.
Everyone was impressed by the handsome young
man who was so deeply in love.

The wedding day finally arrived! The Prince
could not take his eyes off Belle when she
appeared at the top of the grand staircase.
Maurice beamed as he escorted his daughter
down to the Prince.

During the ceremony, Belle read from her favourite book of exciting adventures. "But they don't compare to what I feel every day with you," she told the Prince.

The Prince gave Belle his gift from the village – a blank journal.

"You can fill it with all the adventures we will have together," he said.

After the ceremony, Belle and the Prince walked into the ballroom. The servants had created a spectacular celebration! "Thank you!" said Belle. "But there is so much! I'm not sure our whole household can eat all this food!" she joked.

Mrs Potts and the
other servants just
smiled and ushered
the couple into
the garden ...

... where the entire village was waiting to surprise them!
"I took the liberty of inviting them, on behalf of the
household," said Lumiere.

"It's a magnificent gift!" the Prince exclaimed.
He looked at Belle. "We are truly loved."
"Yes, we are," Belle agreed, beaming.

"Thank you for coming!" the Prince repeated over and over. He couldn't stop smiling. He and Belle were thrilled to welcome everyone into their home.

When the couple shared their first dance, a shout went up from the crowd. "Congratulations!"

As fireworks lit up the night sky, Belle and the Prince
knew that their wedding had been a perfect celebration –
for everyone. With so many friends gathered around them,
it had been the most magical day of all.